JOSÉ AND THE PIRATE CAPTAIN
TOLEDANO

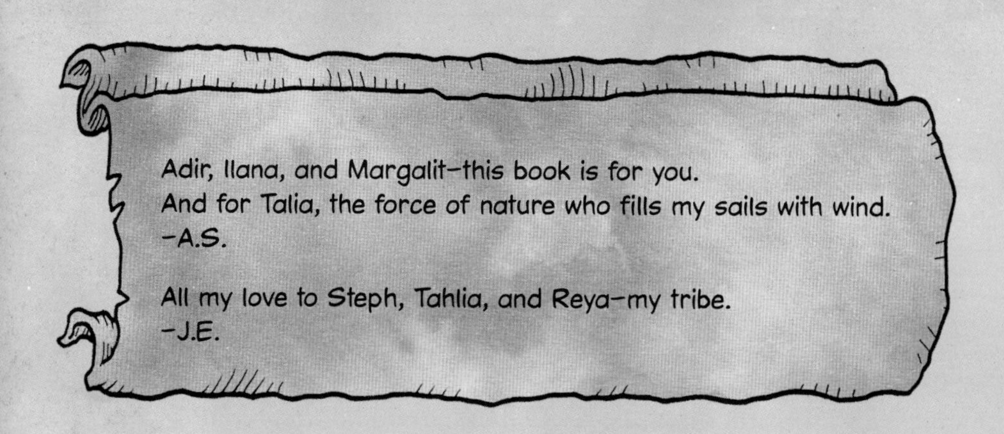

KAR-BEN PUBLISHING®
An imprint of Lerner Publishing Group, Inc.
241 First Avenue North
Minneapolis, MN 55401 USA
Website address: www.karben.com

Main body text set in CCDaveGibbonsLower.
Typeface provided by Comicraft.

Library of Congress Cataloging-in-Publication Data

Names: Shorr, Arnon Z., author. I Edelglass, Joshua M., illustrator.
Title: Jose and the pirate captain / Arnon Z. Shorr ; illustrated by Joshua M. Edelglass.
Description: Minneapolis, MN : Kar-Ben Publishing, [2022] I Audience: Ages 8–12 I Audience: Grades 4–6 I Summary: "Set in the shadows of the Spanish Inquisition, José and the Pirate Captain Toledano is the coming-of-age story of Jose Alfaro, who has a powerful bond with with the mysterious Pirate Captain Toledano"– Provided by publisher.
Identifiers: LCCN 2021014677 (print) I LCCN 2021014678 (ebook) I ISBN 9781728420097 (paperback) I ISBN 9781728446066 I ISBN 9781728444239 (ebook)
Subjects: LCSH: Graphic novels. I CYAC: Graphic novels. I Sea stories. I Pirates–Fiction. I Coming of age–Fiction.
Classification: LCC PZ7.7.S4736 Jo 2022 (print) I LCC PZ7.7.S4736 (ebook) I DDC 741.5/973–dc23

LC record available at https://lccn.loc.gov/2021014677
LC ebook record available at https://lccn.loc.gov/2021014678

Manufactured in the United States of America
1-49120-49289-9/7/2021

JOSÉ AND THE PIRATE CAPTAIN TOLEDANO

Arnon Z. Shorr
Joshua M. Edelglass

KAR-BEN
PUBLISHING

Santo Domingo
1547
STOP!
THIEF!

I'M NOT A THIEF!
I WORKED FOR YOU! YOU OWE ME!

YOU'RE JUST A KID! I PAID YOU A KID'S WAGES --

RRAWRK?!
-- OOF!

I'M NOT JUST A KID!
YOU'RE NOT A THIEF? YOU'RE NOT A KID?
SO WHAT ARE YOU?

YOU'RE AN OVER-EDUCATED FREAK!
THAT'S WHAT!

WHAT DOES HE KNOW?

HE'S JUST JEALOUS.

BECAUSE HE DOESN'T SPEAK FIVE LANGUAGES.

AND BECAUSE HE NEEDS TO HIRE A FOURTEEN-YEAR-OLD TO WRITE HIS LETTERS.

. . . RAN THAT WAY!

HE'S JUST JEALOUS . . .

OOOF!

YOU ARE LATE!
PAPA!

NEXT TIME YOU ARE LATE FOR YOUR LESSONS, YOU WILL NOT BE ALLOWED TO GO TO THE DOCKS FOR A WEEK!

IT'S NOT FAIR, PAPA!

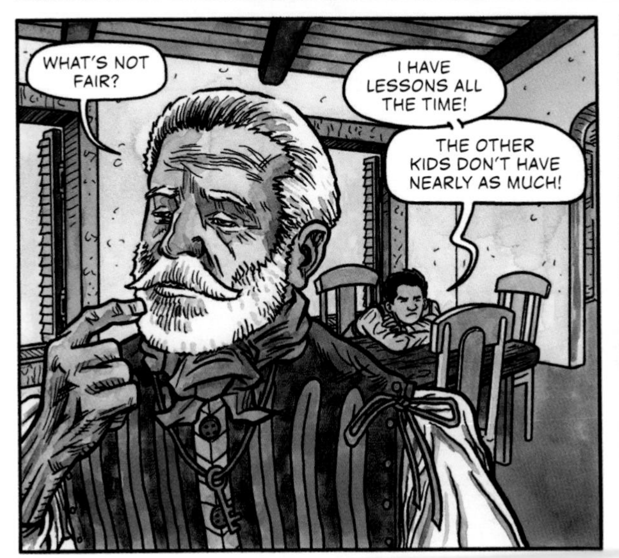
WHAT'S NOT FAIR?
I HAVE LESSONS ALL THE TIME!
THE OTHER KIDS DON'T HAVE NEARLY AS MUCH!

AH! THERE IT IS.
NO ONE LIKES THAT I'M SMART! THAT MERCHANT -- HE CALLED ME AN OVER-EDUCATED FREAK!

ARE YOU EVEN LISTENING TO ME?

I AM YOUR FATHER.
YOU SHOULD BE LISTENING TO ME.

WHAM!

READ. THE SECOND VERSE.
I DON'T WANT TO.

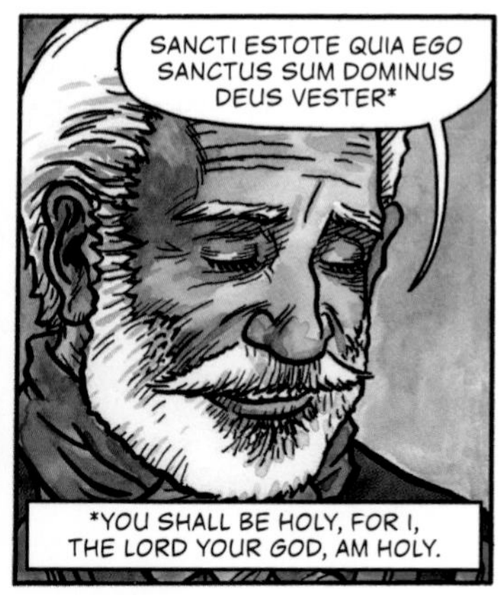
SANCTI ESTOTE QUIA EGO SANCTUS SUM DOMINUS DEUS VESTER*
*YOU SHALL BE HOLY, FOR I, THE LORD YOUR GOD, AM HOLY.

TRANSLATE: SANCTUS!
SANCTUS --
SANTO --
ιερός –
קדוש

HOLY.

GOOD. YOU REMEMBER SOME THINGS.
I HATE THAT I KNOW ALL THAT!
NONE OF THE OTHER KIDS KNOW SO MUCH!

WHAT DOES IT MEAN? TO BE HOLY?

I . . . I DON'T KNOW.

MY BOY, TO BE HOLY . . .
IS TO BE DIFFERENT.

BUT . . . BUT I DON'T WANT TO BE DIFFERENT!
I WANT TO BE LIKE EVERYONE ELSE!
HM.

IT IS TIME.

UH . . . PAPA?

IT IS TIME THAT YOU LEARN WHAT IT REALLY MEANS TO BE HOLY.

KNOCK KNOCK
SEÑOR ALFARO!

NO ONE MUST KNOW OF THIS!
SLAM!

FERDINAND! AN UNEXPECTED SURPRISE! PLEASE, COME IN.
NO, SEÑOR, TOO MUCH TO DO.
TO WHAT DO WE OWE THE --
IT'S THE *SANTA CLARA*!
SHE MET PIRATES ON THE WAY TO MEXICO! THEY HAVE TO STOP HERE FOR REPAIRS!
IS SHE FULLY LADEN?
TONS OF DRY GOODS FROM IBERIA.
AND SETTLERS. TWENTY FAMILIES.
THEY HAD A ROUGH JOURNEY -- THEY'LL WANT TO STAY IN SANTO DOMINGO.
TWENTY FAMILIES! THERE IS NO ROOM!
JOSÉ! IT'S TIME TO PUT YOUR TRAINING TO USE!

GO TO THE TAINO, SPEAK WITH THEIR *CACICA*.
SPEAK IN THEIR LANGUAGE, THE *ARAWAK* WORDS THAT I TAUGHT YOU.
THEY MUST AGREE TO SELL US THEIR LAND, OR THE SETTLERS WILL HAVE NOWHERE TO LIVE!
IF YOU DO THIS, MY BOY, YOU WILL RAISE OUR ESTEEM IN THE GOVERNOR'S EYES.
YOU WILL BE A **HERO** OF THE COLONY.
AND NO ONE CALLS THE HERO A FREAK!

JOSÉ!
WHAT ARE YOU DOING HERE?

ROSA! I COULD ASK YOU THE SAME THING!

I WAS JUST SPEAKING WITH THE *CACICA*. SHE GAVE ME SOME HERBS THAT CAN CURE A FEVER.
THAT REMINDS ME! I'VE GOT SOMETHING FOR YOU!

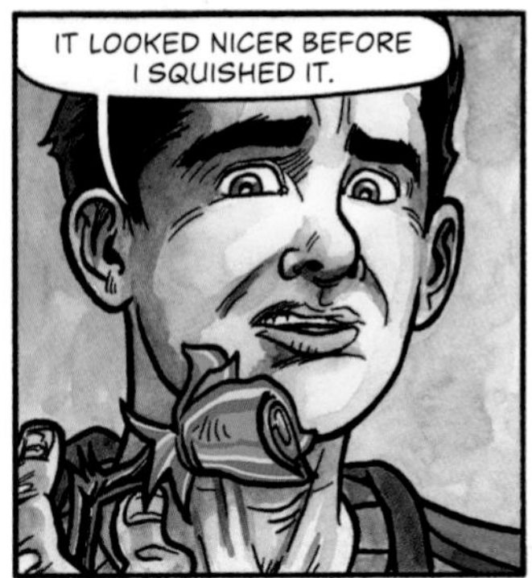
IT LOOKED NICER BEFORE I SQUISHED IT.

TEE-HEE!

IT'S LOVELY, JOSÉ. I'LL HIDE IT SO MY FATHER WON'T FIND IT.

HE STILL DOESN'T LIKE ME?

YOU KNOW HOW HE IS . . .

DID YOU HEAR ABOUT THE *SANTA CLARA*? ATTACKED BY PIRATES!
THAT'S TERRIBLE!
I KNOW! I SAW THE SHIP FROM MY HOUSE -- THE SAILS WERE SHREDDED.
PIRATES! CAN YOU IMAGINE!

IT MUST HAVE BEEN SO EXCITING! I BET THE PIRATE SHIP GOT BLOWN TO PIECES!
IF YOU THINK THAT'S EXCITING, YOU SHOULD LEAVE THE COLONY, BECOME A SAILOR FOR THE SPANISH NAVY.

BUT I'M GOING TO BE IMPORTANT HERE.
I'M CONCLUDING A LAND DEAL FOR MY FATHER! I'M GOING TO MAKE THE TAINO MOVE INLAND TO MAKE ROOM FOR THE NEW SETTLERS.

I TAKE IT BACK -- YOU SHOULD JOIN THE PIRATES, NOT THE NAVY!

ROSA!
SOMETIMES, I THINK THE CACICA CAN CURE ANYTHING WITH THE RIGHT PLANTS. I COME HERE A LOT TO LEARN FROM HER.

DON'T PUSH THEM TOO FAR AWAY.

WHY DOES IT FEEL LIKE I CAN'T DO ANYTHING RIGHT? I KEEP TRYING TO FIT IN, BUT NOTHING WORKS!
PAPA SAID IF I HELP THE COLONY . . .
WHY DOESN'T ANYBODY LIKE ME?

STOP TRYING TO PROVE YOURSELF.
SOME PEOPLE DO LIKE YOU.

I LIKE YOU.

MEANWHILE, IN SANTO DOMINGO . . .
THEY CAME AT US WITH NO MERCY!
GUNS BLAZING!
BUT THEY WERE NO MATCH FOR THE *SANTA CLARA*!
WHY'S THAT, CAPTAIN DE GUZMAN?

BECAUSE GOD FIGHTS ON OUR SIDE!

CAPTAIN DE GUZMAN!

AH, THE GOVERNOR GRACES US WITH HIS PRESENCE!
IT HAS BEEN A LONG TIME, SEÑOR FUENTES!

WE CAME AS SOON AS WE HEARD YOU WASHED UP ON OUR SHORE!
THIS IS SEÑOR ALFARO, TREASURER TO THE COLONY. HE WILL ARRANGE LODGING FOR YOUR SAILORS AND WILL MAKE SURE YOUR SHIP IS REPAIRED.
IF THE CROWN WILL REIMBURSE OUR EXPENSES, YOUR SHIP WILL BE REPAIRED QUICKLY.

NOT TOO QUICKLY, I HOPE.
GOD SENT THOSE PIRATES TO ATTACK MY SHIP. HE HAS PLANS FOR ME IN SANTO DOMINGO.

PLEASE! JOIN ME AT MY TABLE.
KICK!

FROM A YOUNG AGE, I WAS TAUGHT THE IMPORTANCE OF THE PURITY OF THE CATHOLIC FAITH.
CAPTAIN DE GUZMAN'S FATHER WAS A GRAND INQUISITOR!

HERESY MUST BE EXTINGUISHED FOR THE TRUE FAITH TO THRIVE.
DO YOU NOT AGREE, SEÑOR ALFARO?
OH . . . OF COURSE, CAPTAIN.

BUT IT'S NOT ENOUGH TO CONVERT THE HERETIC. NO . . .
SOME PEOPLE ARE TOO DIFFERENT.

HERESY IS IN THEIR BLOOD.

ARE YOU A GAMBLING MAN, GOVERNOR?
ONLY IF I LIKE THE ODDS.
ARE THERE HERETICS IN SANTO DOMINGO?
CERTAINLY NOT, CAPTAIN!

THEN I PROPOSE A WAGER.

I BET YOU TEN PIECES OF EIGHT THAT I WILL FIND A HERETIC IN SANTO DOMINGO BEFORE MY SHIP IS REPAIRED.
IT'S A DEAL!
YOU MAY BEGIN YOUR INQUISITION IMMEDIATELY!

BACK AT THE TAINO VILLAGE . . .
STEP IN HERE. THE *CACICA* WILL SEE YOU.*
*SPEAKING IN ARAWAK, THE LANGUAGE OF THE TAINO.

THANK YOU!

YOU SPEAK ARAWAK?

I LEARN WORDS FROM FATHER. NO SPEAK GOOD.
MY NAME JOSÉ ALFARO.

I WILL SPEAK YOUR LANGUAGE, JOSÉ. IT WILL BE EASIER FOR BOTH OF US.
BUT I AM GRATEFUL TO YOUR FATHER. HE IS A WISE MAN FOR TEACHING YOU YOUR NEIGHBOR'S LANGUAGE.
COME. YOU BRING A MESSAGE FROM THE COLONY?

IT'S THE TERMS OF THE LAND DEAL.
LET ME SEE.
WE WERE HOPING YOU WOULD SIGN IT.

WHAT TREACHERY IS THIS?!

THIS DEAL IS AN OUTRAGE!
WHERE WILL WE FISH? YOU WOULD PUSH US A DAY'S HIKE FROM THE WATER?

CACICA! ARE YOU OKAY?
PLEASE --
THERE ARE MORE SETTLERS COMING --
WHERE WILL THEY LIVE?

IF I RETURN WITHOUT YOUR SIGNATURE --

SHOULD I TAKE HIM AWAY?
COUGH

LEAVE HIM BE. WE ARE NOT DONE.

COUGH

GRANDMOTHER?
HUSH, DEAR BOY.
I DID NOT MEAN TO DISTURB YOUR REST.

HE IS THE SON OF MY SON. SICK WITH SMALLPOX.
HIS PARENTS DIED FROM THE DISEASE.

AS DID HALF OF OUR NATION.

I'M SORRY, CACICA.
IF I HAD KNOWN IT WAS A BAD TIME --

IT IS ALWAYS A BAD TIME FOR A DEAL SUCH AS THIS.
SCRUNCH

DO YOU KNOW THE GIRL WHO WAS JUST HERE? ROSA?
YES! SHE IS MY FRIEND.
SHE IS DIFFERENT.

YOU ARE DIFFERENT TOO.

WHY DOES EVERYONE KEEP TELLING ME THAT?
BECAUSE IT IS TRUE. AND BECAUSE YOU SHOULD KNOW IT.
BUT I DON'T WANT TO BE DIFFERENT.
THAT IS WHAT YOUR TRIBE WANTS. THEY DON'T VALUE DIFFERENCE.

YOU KNOW WHAT YOU SHOULD WANT?
A BETTER TRIBE.

YOU SHOULD WANT A BETTER TRIBE.

ROSA WAS RIGHT --

I SHOULD BECOME A SAILOR!
WITH ALL THE LANGUAGES I KNOW . . .
I COULD BE REALLY VALUABLE TO CAPTAIN DE GUZMAN!

PAPA! I WANT TO TELL YOU SOMETHING! I'M GOING TO JOIN DE GUZMAN'S CREW ON THE *SANTA CLARA*!
PAPA?
DON'T BE A FOOL.
DID THEY SIGN IT?

PAPA! WHAT ARE YOU --
MY BOY!
DID THEY SIGN?
THE *CACICA* REFUSED!

WE ARE IN MORE TROUBLE THAN I FEARED.

WHAT'S GOING ON?
STAY AWAY FROM DE GUZMAN.
HE IS DANGEROUS.
CREEEK!

DANGEROUS? WHAT ARE YOU TALKING ABOUT?
THIS WILL EXPLAIN A LOT, MY BOY.

WE LEFT PORTUGAL WHEN YOUR MOTHER DIED.
CLICK
I THOUGHT I WAS BORN HERE!

I WANTED TO BURY HER IN THE MANNER OF OUR FAITH.
OUR FAITH? BUT WE'RE --

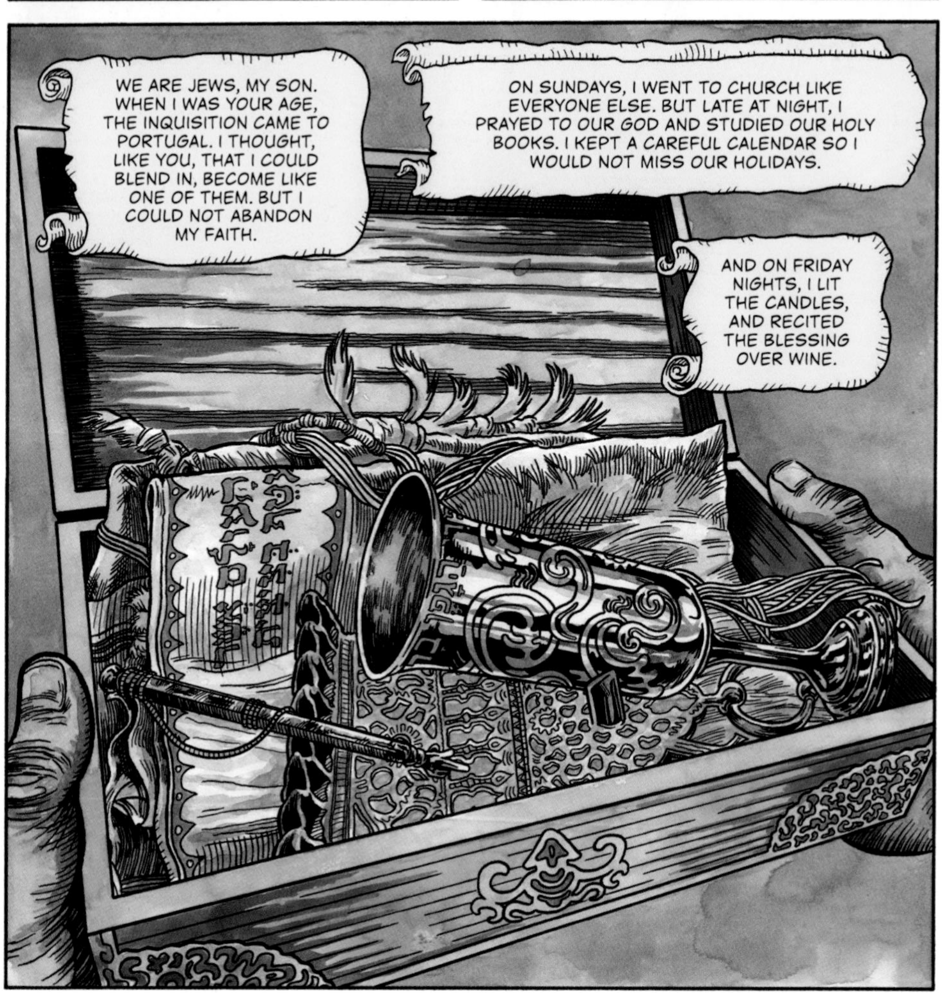
WE ARE JEWS, MY SON. WHEN I WAS YOUR AGE, THE INQUISITION CAME TO PORTUGAL. I THOUGHT, LIKE YOU, THAT I COULD BLEND IN, BECOME LIKE ONE OF THEM. BUT I COULD NOT ABANDON MY FAITH.
ON SUNDAYS, I WENT TO CHURCH LIKE EVERYONE ELSE. BUT LATE AT NIGHT, I PRAYED TO OUR GOD AND STUDIED OUR HOLY BOOKS. I KEPT A CAREFUL CALENDAR SO I WOULD NOT MISS OUR HOLIDAYS.
AND ON FRIDAY NIGHTS, I LIT THE CANDLES, AND RECITED THE BLESSING OVER WINE.

WHEN YOUR MOTHER DIED, I TORE MY CLOTHES IN THE REQUIRED MANNER.
SOMEBODY SAW ME AND REPORTED ME TO THE LOCAL INQUISITOR.
I BOOKED PASSAGE FOR US ON A SHIP BOUND FOR THE NEW WORLD.
I HOPED AN OCEAN FULL OF WATER WOULD KEEP THE INQUISITION'S FIRES AWAY.
I MADE A PROMISE BEFORE GOD THAT I WOULD PROTECT YOU FROM THEM, AND THAT WHEN YOU WERE OLD ENOUGH, I WOULD TEACH YOU ABOUT OUR FAITH.

BUT YOU DIDN'T TEACH ME ABOUT IT!
I'M NOT . . .
I CAN'T BE . . .

YOU ARE A JEW, JOSÉ.
AND IF YOU FELT OUT OF PLACE BEFORE, IT WILL GET WORSE FOR US NOW.
SNAP!

YOUR HERO, DE GUZMAN -- HE IS AN INQUISITOR!
THE INQUISITION HAS COME TO SANTO DOMINGO!

WITHOUT THE LAND DEAL, THE GOVERNOR WILL NOT PROTECT US FROM HIM.
BUT YOU'RE THE COLONIAL TREASURER! YOUR WORK IS SO IMPORTANT!

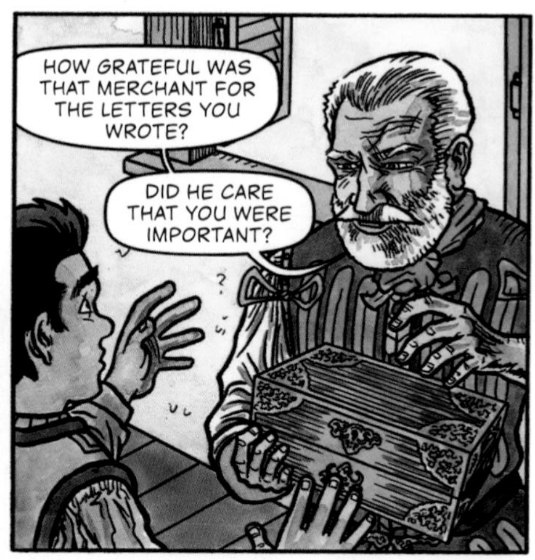
HOW GRATEFUL WAS THAT MERCHANT FOR THE LETTERS YOU WROTE?
DID HE CARE THAT YOU WERE IMPORTANT?

WHAT DID HE CALL YOU?
A FREAK?

KNOCK
KNOCK
KNOCK

CRASH!

STAY CALM.

AH, GOOD. THE BOY IS HERE.
SAVES US SOME TROUBLE.

CAPTAIN DE GUZMAN! HAVE THE WORKERS STOPPED REPAIRING YOUR SHIP?

YOU GOT SLOPPY, JEW. YOU THOUGHT WE WOULDN'T FIND YOU IN THE NEW WORLD.
WHAT ARE YOU TALKING ABOUT?

DON'T TOY WITH ME!

THERE'S THE PROOF!

GRAB HIM!

RUN!

OOOF!

DON'T LET HIM GET AWAY!

WHAT DO I DO?
WHERE DO I GO?

YOU CANNOT STAY HERE, JOSÉ.

IF THE COLONISTS LEARNED YOU WERE HERE, WE WOULD SUFFER FOR IT. BESIDES --
WE ARE NOT YOUR PEOPLE.
I . . . I DON'T EVEN KNOW WHO I AM ANYMORE.
YOU ARE WHO YOU HAVE ALWAYS BEEN.
IT IS YOUR TRIBE THAT YOU MUST FIND.

PLEASE ACCEPT THIS SUPPLY OF FOOD. IT WILL LAST YOU A FEW DAYS.

A FEW DAYS? THEN WHAT?
THERE IS A SHIP.
IN A COVE, NOT FAR FROM HERE.

IT APPEARED TWO NIGHTS AGO, IN SOME DISREPAIR.
GET ABOARD BEFORE IT LEAVES.
GO WHERE THEY TAKE YOU.
FIND YOUR TRIBE.

A SHIP . . .
WHAT FLAG DID IT FLY?

IT FLEW NO FLAG AT ALL.

The Lagish

AND THAT'S ALL WE'RE WAITING FOR?
JUST THE SAILS. EVERYTHING ELSE IS REPAIRED.

IF I KNEW HOW TO SEW, I'D OFFER TO HELP.
THE THOUGHT OF YOU WITH A NEEDLE AND THREAD!
HA!

THUNK

YOU TWO BETTER GO BELOW. DINNER'S GETTING COLD.
I'LL TAKE OVER YOUR WATCH.
THANK YOU, SIR!

CHICKEN AGAIN!
AYE, SALMAN STOLE THREE HENS FROM THE TOWN.
ALL IN A DAY'S WORK, BOYS!
SEE? THERE'S GOOD THAT COMES FROM BEING STUCK AN EXTRA DAY.
SHOULD I BRING SOME TO THE CAPTAIN?
DON'T BOTHER. CAPTAIN WON'T EAT WHAT WE EAT, MOST O' THE TIME.

OVEREDUCATED FREAK!
YOU GOT SLOPPY, JEW!
I LIKE YOU.
LEARN WHAT IT MEANS TO BE HOLY.
FIND YOUR TRIBE!
GASP!
WHAT WAS THAT?

WHAT WAS WHAT?
I HEARD A VOICE.
DOWN THERE.
WELL LOOK AT THIS.
TAKE HIM ON DECK. I'LL GET THE CAPTAIN.
CAPTAIN TOLEDANO!
I AM EATING.
WE CAUGHT A STOWAWAY!

SHOW ME.

QUIT YER FIGHTING, SHARK BAIT!
I'M NOT FIGHTING!
DON'T GET TOO CLOSE -- HE SMELLS OF FILTH.

JUST A CUB.

BUT A STOWAWAY, NONETHELESS.
WHY DID YOU SNEAK ABOARD MY SHIP?

I . . . I HAD NOWHERE ELSE TO GO!

A STOWAWAY BELONGS AT THE BOTTOM OF THE SEA!
THIS IS A PIRATE SHIP, NOT AN ALMS HOUSE.

I . . . I CAN BE A PIRATE!

HA HA HA HA HA HA
HA HA HA HA HA HA HA HA HA HA

I CAN BE USEFUL! I SPEAK FIVE LANGUAGES! AND I KNOW HOW TO READ AND --

OOOH! THE STOWAWAY CAN READ!
WHEN HAS THAT EVER HELPED ANYONE?
ENOUGH.

THE BOY IS RIGHT. HIS SKILLS MAY BE USEFUL.
BUT HIS TIMING IS . . . UNFORTUNATE.

YOU SEE, YOUNG MAN, WE ARE IN PURSUIT OF AN ENEMY. AN ENEMY I HAVE BEEN TRAILING SINCE BEFORE YOU WERE BORN.

THEN LET ME FIGHT WITH YOU!
THIS IS NO TIME TO TAKE IN A STRAY.
I CAN SWING A SWORD!
YOU CAN READ AND YOU CAN SWING A SWORD?
YOU'LL SWING FROM THE YARDARM, YOU LITERATE FREAK!

I'M NOT A FREAK!

I JUST . . . KNOW THINGS.
TSK.

GET RID OF HIM.

HOLD!

THAT'S . . . THAT'S MINE.
IT WAS MY FATHER'S . . .

PLEASE . . . IT'S ALL I HAVE LEFT.

TAKE HIM TO THE BRIG!

NO!
PLEASE!
BUT CAPT --
THAT'S AN ORDER!

HE'S A LUCKY KID, Y'KNOW THAT?
YEAH. LUCKY KID.
I WONDER WHAT THE CAPTAIN'S GONNA DO WITH HIM?

SLAM
YOU EVER SEEN A STOWAWAY WHO WASN'T FED TO THE SHARKS?

GUARDS!
COME UP HERE!

AYE, CAPTAIN!
AYE!

STAND UP, YOUNG MAN, AND TELL ME.
WHERE DID YOU STEAL THAT CUP?

SNIFF
I DIDN'T STEAL IT. M-MY FATHER, HE . . . HE . . .

ARE YOU A JEW?

I JUST FOUND OUT. MY FATHER KEPT IT FROM ME. BUT THEN SOLDIERS CAME. THEY TOOK HIM . . .

ES CUZIR TE ABIKA!*
*THIS IS YOUR FATHER'S CUP!

YOU SPEAK LADINO?
YOUR FATHER DIDN'T KEEP EVERYTHING FROM YOU. IT IS OUR LANGUAGE.
OUR LANGUAGE?
I WILL SHARE WITH YOU A SECRET -- A SECRET THAT NO ONE ON THIS SHIP KNOWS.

I, TOO, AM A JEW.

BUT . . . BUT YOU'RE A PIRATE!

YO EXPULSO DE TOLEDO.*
*I WAS EXPELLED FROM TOLEDO.

DE GUZMAN --
TFU!

-- DE GUZMAN QUEMADA ABI AL POSTE.*
*DE GUZMAN BURNED MY FATHER AT THE STAKE.

BUT DE GUZMAN IS YOUNGER THAN YOU -- I SAW HIM!
DE GUZMAN THE SON --
AS BAD AS HIS FATHER.
YOU SAW HIM? WHERE?
IN SANTO DOMINGO. HE WAS REPAIRING HIS SHIP . . .

YOU'RE THE PIRATE!

HIS SHIP, THE *SANTA CLARA*, IT WAS ALL SHOT UP WHEN THEY CAME INTO PORT!
YOU DID THAT!
THEY LANDED A LUCKY SHOT. CRIPPLED US BEFORE WE COULD FINISH THEM OFF.
IS THE SHIP STILL THERE?
WHEN DO THEY DEPART?

YOU COULD CATCH THEM! THE SHIP WAS BADLY DAMAGED -- IT MUST STILL BE THERE!
NO. THE CANNONS IN SANTO DOMINGO -- THEY PROTECT THE HARBOR. I CANNOT ATTACK UNTIL THE SHIP RETURNS TO SEA.
FOR FIFTEEN YEARS, I HAVE PURSUED DE GUZMAN AND HIS ACCURSED SHIP.
FIRST IN THE MEDITERRANEAN, THEN THE WEST AFRICAN COAST. I LOST TRACK OF HIM FOR A TIME.
THEN I HEARD HE HAD CROSSED THE GREAT OCEAN.
ALL OF THAT BECAUSE OF HIS FATHER?
THE SPANISH BUILT THEIR FLEET WITH THE WEALTH THAT THEY STOLE FROM MY PEOPLE.
SO I STEAL IT BACK!

LET ME JOIN YOU! TEACH ME HOW TO BE A PIRATE!

STOWAWAYS MUST BE PUNISHED, SO YOU WILL SPEND THE NIGHT HERE.
BUT TOMORROW . . .

TOMORROW YOU WILL RISE AS A PIRATE OF THE *LAQISH*.

I WILL ALERT THE QUARTERMASTER TO PREPARE FOR YOUR TRAINING.
WHAT ABOUT MY FATHER'S CUP?

WHAT GOOD IS IT TO YOU IF YOU DON'T KNOW WHAT TO DO WITH IT?
COME TO ME FOR LESSONS. WHEN YOU HAVE LEARNED ENOUGH, THE CUP WILL BE YOURS AGAIN.

YOU WHAT?
HE IS A STOWAWAY!
AND I AM A CAPTAIN.
MY APOLOGIES, SIR. HIS TRAINING WILL BEGIN AS SOON AS HIS STRENGTH HAS RETURNED.
JOSÉ! TIME FOR A LESSON!
IT MEANS "THE LORD OUR GOD, THE LORD IS ONE."
I KNOW WHAT IT MEANS. I'VE STUDIED THIS BEFORE.
BUT NOT AS A JEW! THE UNITY OF GOD IS CENTRAL TO OUR --
CAN I GO BACK ON DECK NOW? I'M LEARNING SWORDSMANSHIP TODAY!
THIS ISN'T WHAT I EXPECTED.
WHAT GOOD IS A SWORD IF IT IS NOT SHARP?
JOSÉ!
FROM GOD TO MOSES, THEN FROM HIM TO JOSHUA, THEN TO THE ELDERS, THEN THE PROPHETS, TO THE MEN OF THE GREAT ASSEMBLY . . . NOW YOU SEE HOW LONG THE CHAIN OF TRADITION STRETCHES, AND HOW FRAGILE IT IS.
ALL IT TAKES IS FOR ONE LINK IN THE CHAIN TO BREAK, AND THE WHOLE THING IS GONE.
THAT IS WHAT THE INQUISITION IS TRYING TO DO TO US.
פרקי
אבות
JOSÉ? ARE YOU LISTENING?
SORRY, I CUT MY FINGER ON A SWORD . . .

SO, BY CHECKING THE SUN'S NOONTIME POSITION AGAINST THIS CHART, WE CAN PINPOINT OUR EXACT LOCATION ON THE MAP!
YOU ARE UNUSUALLY SMART.
JOSÉ! IT'S TIME!
WHY IS HE THE CAPTAIN'S FAVORITE ALL OF A SUDDEN?
BUT IF GOD KNOWS EVERYTHING, WHY DOES HE LET THINGS LIKE THE INQUISITION HAPPEN?
THAT IS INDEED A DIFFICULT QUESTION,
BUT I BELIEVE MAIMONIDES ADDRESSES IT HERE, IN THE ELEVENTH PRINCIPLE.
VERY GOOD, JOSÉ!
IT'S A LONG WAY DOWN FROM HERE!
KEEP CLIMBING!
YOU'RE ALMOST THERE!
WHY ARE WE PLAYIN' GAMES WITH THAT KID?

CAPTAIN! A WORD?
SLAM

THE DOOR IS CLOSED!

I AM SORRY, SIR, BUT THIS IS A DELICATE MATTER THAT SHOULD NOT WAIT.
WHAT DO YOU HAVE THERE?

IT IS NOT OF YOUR CONCERN.
WHAT'S GOING ON?

IT'S ABOUT THE BOY, JOSÉ. THE OTHERS HAVE NOTICED YOUR **INTEREST** IN HIM.
IT IS MY RIGHT AS CAPTAIN. AND IT IS **YOUR** JOB TO REMIND THEM OF THAT.

I MADE IT!

THE BOY HAS BEEN TRAINING FOR JUST A FEW WEEKS, AND HIS TRAINING IS INTERRUPTED BY YOUR LESSONS. HE IS NOT READY FOR BATTLE. IF WE COME UPON A SHIP . . .
HOW MUCH TRAINING DID YOU HAVE WHEN YOU SAW YOUR FIRST FIGHT?
THAT IS WHEN REAL TRAINING BEGINS, ANYWAY.
BUT OUR MEN ARE CONCERNED --
IF HE SHOULD MAKE A MISTAKE --

YOU'VE SAID ENOUGH. I WILL MAKE SURE THE BOY IS NOT UNDERFOOT.

BUT KNOW THIS, AND MAKE IT CLEAR TO THE CREW. JOSÉ IS A PIRATE OF THE *LAQISH*.
A SAIL! A SAIL!

I SPOTTED A SAIL!
ANOTHER SHIP!

IT IS A CARAVEL!
WHAT ARE HER COLORS?
BLUE FLAGS --
SPANISH MERCHANTS.
GOOD.

AND SHE SITS LOW IN THE WATER.

THEN THERE IS MUCH TO PLUNDER.
PREPARE FOR BATTLE!

ALL HANDS TO QUARTERS!
AYE, SIR!
SOUND THE BELL!
I'LL GET A SWORD!
NOT TODAY.

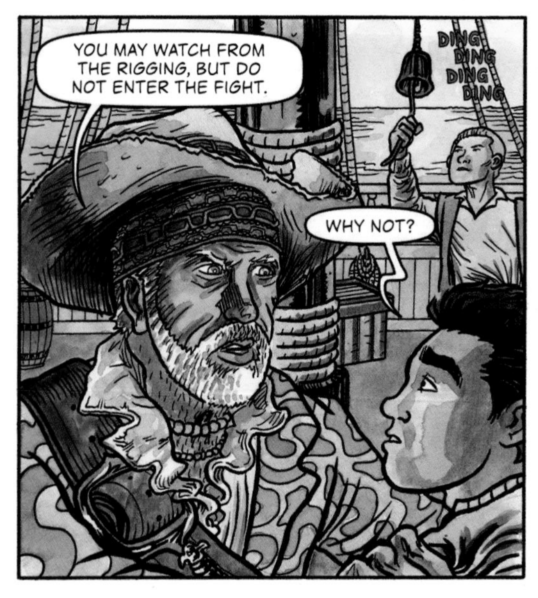
DING DING DING DING
YOU MAY WATCH FROM THE RIGGING, BUT DO NOT ENTER THE FIGHT.
WHY NOT?

THERE ARE PIRATES ON THIS SHIP WHO STILL SEE YOU AS A STOWAWAY.

SET COURSE TO INTERCEPT!

THIS IS SO UNFAIR.

I'VE BEEN HERE A MONTH! I'M ONE OF THEM NOW!
FWOOSH

WHOA . . . HERE IT COMES . . .

FIRE!

BOOM

BOOM
BOOM
BOOM

THIS IS IT.
AWAY THE HOOKS!

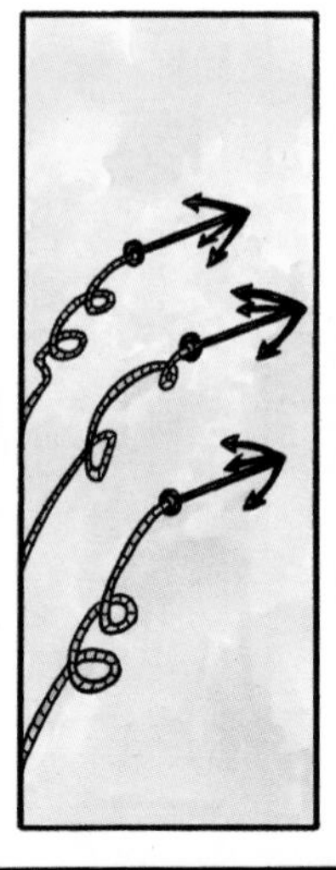

AQISH
WHOA!

CHAAAARGE!
LEAVE THEIR CAPTAIN TO ME!

OH, HELP!

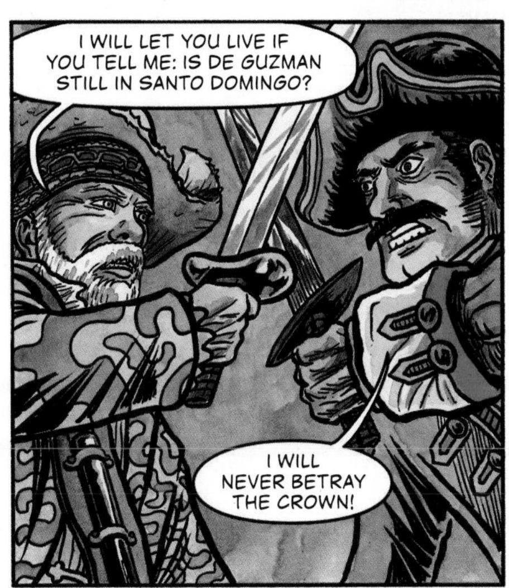
I WILL LET YOU LIVE IF YOU TELL ME: IS DE GUZMAN STILL IN SANTO DOMINGO?
I WILL NEVER BETRAY THE CROWN!

CAN'T . . .
HOLD . . .

DOCTOR!
I'M COMING!
OKAY! I YIELD!

DE GUZMAN?
HE IS IN SANTO DOMINGO!
BUT THE REPAIRS ON HIS SHIP ARE NEAR COMPLETE! THE *SANTA CLARA* WILL SAIL AGAIN SOON!

YOU WILL SAIL EAST, AND NEVER RETURN.

AAAHHHH!

IF I SEE YOU AGAIN, I WILL TURN YOUR SHIP INTO A REEF.

OOF!

OH! MY HAND! IT'S BROKEN!

MY HAND!
I CAN'T WORK WITHOUT MY HAND!
I'M SO SORRY!

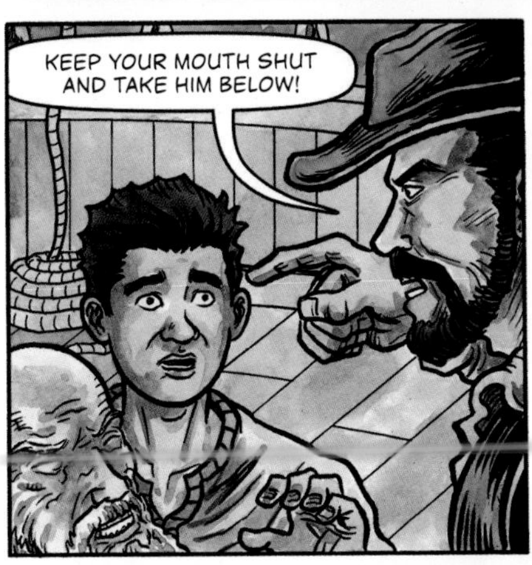
KEEP YOUR MOUTH SHUT AND TAKE HIM BELOW!

I KNEW HE'D BE TROUBLE.
WE SHOULD HAVE TOSSED HIM OVERBOARD RIGHT WHEN WE CAUGHT HIM.

CAPTAIN! WE'VE TAKEN ALL WE CAN. THE CARAVEL IS NEARLY EMPTY.
CUT THEM LOOSE. THEN SET A COURSE FOR SANTO DOMINGO.
WE'RE GOING BACK?
THE *SANTA CLARA* IS ABOUT TO DEPART.
WHAT ABOUT THE BOY?

I WILL DEAL WITH HIM.

YAAAAGH!
DON'T TOUCH!
IT HURTS!
TELL ME WHAT TO DO! TELL ME HOW TO HELP!

WHY DON'T YOU GET THE DOCTOR?
OH, YEAH! I'M THE DOCTOR!
HA! HA! HA! HA! OW!

BACK OFF, STOWAWAY!
HERE. MY SHARE OF THE ALE.
GLUG

I'M NOT A STOWAWAY!
I AM A PIRATE!

WATCH YER TONGUE, BOY!
YOU CRIPPLED OUR DOCTOR!

IF THE CAPTAIN HAD THROWN YOU OVERBOARD . . .
WHAT DOES HE SEE IN YOU, ANYWAY?
NONE OF US GETS PRIVATE LESSONS.
AND WE JOINED THE CREW WITHOUT SNEAKING!

I . . . THE CAPTAIN . . . WE'RE, WE'RE BOTH --
ENOUGH!

DROP HIM.
OOF!

I WILL NOT HAVE SUCH BEHAVIOR ON THIS SHIP. YOU ARE PIRATES OF THE *LAQISH*.
ALL OF YOU.
WE ARE SAILING TOWARDS DANGER, SO SHARPEN YOUR BLADES AND SWALLOW YOUR PRIDE.

JOSÉ! I WILL SPEAK WITH YOU.
NOW.

WE HAVE NO TIME FOR THESE GAMES, JOSÉ!
SLAM!

IT WASN'T MY FAULT!

JUST SIT.

YOU SAY YOU ARE A PIRATE?
THAT MAY BE TRUE. BUT THAT IS NOT ALL YOU ARE.
BUT IT'S ALL I WANT TO BE!
TSK. YOU ARE A JEW, WHETHER YOU LIKE IT OR NOT. YOU ARE DIFFERENT.
WE ARE DIFFERENT.

WHAT DOES THAT EVEN MEAN?!

WE PLUNDER FOR SOMETHING GREATER THAN GOLD.

WE ARE RETURNING TO SANTO DOMINGO.
THE SANTA CLARA?
SHE IS ABOUT TO SET SAIL.
LIKE ALL SPANISH NAVY CAPTAINS, DE GUZMAN WILL FILE HIS ROUTE WITH THE HARBORMASTER.
IF WE CAN STEAL THE HARBORMASTER'S LOG . . .
THEN WE'LL KNOW WHERE SHE'S GOING! WE CAN AMBUSH HER! WE CAN GET DE GUZMAN!

AH, YOU SEE?
YOU ARE NOT INTERESTED IN THE TREASURE SHE CARRIES.
BUT YOU HEAR THAT STILL, SMALL VOICE THAT COMMANDS YOU:

"JUSTICE, JUSTICE YOU SHALL PURSUE!"

THAT MAKES YOU DIFFERENT.
NOW, REVENGE ISN'T EXACTLY JUSTICE . . . BUT WHAT ELSE CAN WE DO? FOR WHAT DE GUZMAN'S FATHER DID TO MY FAMILY.
FOR WHAT DE GUZMAN DID TO YOUR FATHER . . .

MY FATHER . . .
DO YOU THINK . . . MAYBE . . . IF HE'S STILL ALIVE . . . MAYBE WE CAN RESCUE HIM?
I AM SORRY, JOSÉ. WE CANNOT RISK IT.
IF WE RESCUE YOUR FATHER FROM THE INQUISITION, THE OTHERS WILL FIGURE OUT WHO YOU ARE.

AND IT WOULD NOT TAKE LONG FOR THEM TO FIND ME OUT AS WELL.

BUT WHY CAN'T I COME WITH YOU? I CAN GUIDE YOU --

WE WILL BE BACK BEFORE DAWN.
DON'T GET INTO TROUBLE!
YOU WILL HAVE YOUR CHANCE TO PROVE YOURSELF. JUST NOT TONIGHT.

IF YOU SEE MY FATHER --
TAKE HEART, JOSÉ -- WHEN WE STRIKE THE *SANTA CLARA*, YOU WILL FIGHT BY MY SIDE!

I CAN'T JUST SIT HERE.

IF PAPA IS ALIVE, I NEED TO SAVE HIM.

THIS IS IT.

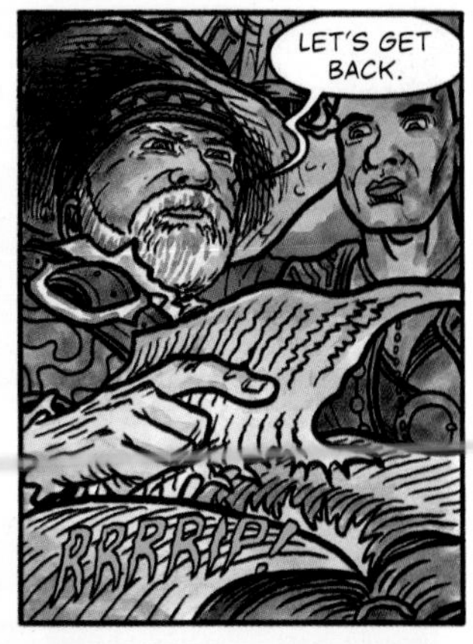
LET'S GET BACK.
RRRRIP!

SLOSH
SLOSH
SLOSH
IF PAPA IS OUT THERE, I BETTER BRING HIM BACK BEFORE THE PIRATES RETURN.

I HOPE HE'S HERE . . .

PAPA!

IF WE HURRY, WE'LL BE BACK AT THE SHIP BEFORE DAWN!

HALT!

OUR QUARREL IS NOT WITH YOU! WE WILL NOT SHED YOUR BLOOD IF YOU LET US GO.

I WILL LET THEM GO.
BUT NOT YOU.

YOUR QUARREL IS WITH ME.

YOU!
STOP!

BUT THE CAPTAIN --
BETTER TO LOSE ONE CAPTAIN THAN HALF OUR CREW.

TRAITOR!
JEW.

I'M TELLING YOU, IT SOUNDED LIKE TROUBLE BY THE HARBOR!
NO WAY YOU CAN HEAR ANYTHING FROM THAT FAR AWAY.

I THOUGHT . . . I THOUGHT I HEARD MY SON!
PAPA? YOU DID HEAR ME!

I'VE COME TO TAKE YOU OUT OF HERE!
I AM WEAK, JOSÉ. I HOPED YOU HAD LEFT THE ISLAND.
I DID! I FOUND A SHIP! I JOINED THEIR CREW! I AM A PIRATE!

A PIRATE?
MY BOY, YOU ARE A PIRATE?

I HID OUR IDENTITY FROM YOU, BUT I THOUGHT I COULD TEACH YOU OUR VALUES.

AND WHAT WAS IT FOR? HIDING DID NOT KEEP US SAFE. THE INQUISITION FOUND US IN THE END. AND YOU ARE NOW A PIRATE, OF ALL GHASTLY THINGS.

BUT, PAPA! YOU DON'T UNDERSTAND --
I DO UNDERSTAND.
I DO.
JOSÉ, ARE YOU FREE? ON THE SHIP, WITH THOSE . . . THOSE SAILORS. CAN YOU TELL THEM THAT YOU ARE A JEW? DO THEY ACCEPT YOU FOR WHO YOU ARE?

NO . . .
BUT --

BUT THE CAPTAIN --
HE'S AN OLD JEW FROM SPAIN! HE SAW YOUR CUP, SO HE KNEW WHAT I WAS.
HE'S BEEN TEACHING ME!

THAT MAY . . .
MAY BE ENOUGH . . .
UGH
PAPA!
WHAT DID THEY DO TO YOU?

WHAT DID THEY DO?
IT'S WHAT THEY DID NOT DO THAT MATTERS.
THEY DID NOT BRING ME WATER FOR DAYS. THEY LEFT ME WITHOUT FOOD FOR A WEEK.
IF NOT FOR YOUR FRIEND, ROSA, I WOULD BE LONG DEAD.

I'LL GET YOU OUT OF HERE.
NO . . .
YOU SHOULD RUN. GO BACK TO YOUR SHIP.

JOSÉ?

YOU MUST HIDE!
ROSA?

THE GUARDS ARE BRINGING A NEW PRISONER!

CLICK

COME OFF IT, YOU'RE FAKING!
HE ISN'T FAKING -- I THINK HE BROKE HIS LEG!

HERE IS THE KEY, SIR.
GIMME THAT!
YOU SHOULDN'T BE HANDLING THE KEYS, GIRL.
JUST TRYING TO HELP.

GET IN THERE, SCUM!

CAN YOU BELIEVE IT?
TWO JEWS IN OUR JAIL AT THE SAME TIME!

MIGHT BE A COLONY RECORD.
NOT A RECORD I'D BRAG ABOUT.

THEY WON'T BE GONE FOR LONG.

CAPTAIN TOLEDANO?
NNNNGGHH

JOSÉ?
YOU ARE NOT ON THE SHIP?
YOU TAUGHT ME TO PURSUE JUSTICE, SO I CAME TO RESCUE MY FATHER!
NOT SO LOUD!

YOUR FATHER?
SEÑOR ALFARO, YOU TAUGHT YOUR SON WELL.

WHAT HAPPENED TO YOU?
THE QUARTERMASTER -- HE RATTED ME OUT!
HE MUST HAVE HEARD US TALKING!
WE SHOULD HAVE BEEN MORE CAREFUL.
NO!

DO NOT HIDE.
I HID. YOU DO NOT HAVE TO.

I SHOWED MY SON OUR FEAR. YOU CAN SHOW HIM OUR PRIDE.

IF THE GUARDS HEARD YOU . . .
UGH.
PAPA!

NNNN . . .

GO, MY SON.
BEFORE THEY RETURN.
BUT, PAPA --
HONOR YOUR FATHER, JOSÉ.
OBEY HIS COMMAND.

I LIKE THIS PIRATE.

BE PROUD, JOSÉ.
I LOVE YOU, PAPA!

GO TO THE TAINO VILLAGE
ASK THE *CACICA* TO HEAL HIS LEG!
YOU HAVE TO!
THEY'RE COMING!
UGH. MY LEG . . . I CANNOT RUN.
I THINK I HEARD THEM! OVER THERE!

DID YOU SEE THEM?
I SAID I HEARD THEM!
CAPTAIN DE GUZMAN WILL NOT BE HAPPY.
COME ON, LET'S GO BACK. WE STILL HAVE ALFARO. DE GUZMAN STILL WINS HIS BET.

YOUR FATHER IS RIGHT.
WE DO OURSELVES NO SERVICE BY HIDING.

WHEN THE *SANTA CLARA* AND HER CAPTAIN LIE ON THE OCEAN FLOOR, I WILL DECLARE THE *LAQISH* A HAVEN ON THE SEAS.
WE WILL NOT HAVE TO HIDE ANYMORE.

YOU'LL TELL THE OTHER PIRATES THAT YOU'RE A JEW?
WE BOTH WILL.
BUT ONLY IF WE CAN GET BACK TO THE SHIP . . .

WHERE IS
EVERYONE?

HELLO?
ARE YOU SURE THIS IS A GOOD IDEA?
MMMMMMHH?

CACICA! I'M SO SORRY TO DISTURB YOU, BUT WE NEED YOUR HELP! MY FRIEND'S LEG --

ARE YOU OKAY?

I CANNOT HELP.
REMEMBER, WHEN I HAD NOWHERE TO GO, YOU TOLD ME TO FIND MY TRIBE?
WELL, I FOUND HIM.
ROSA SAID YOU WOULD HELP!

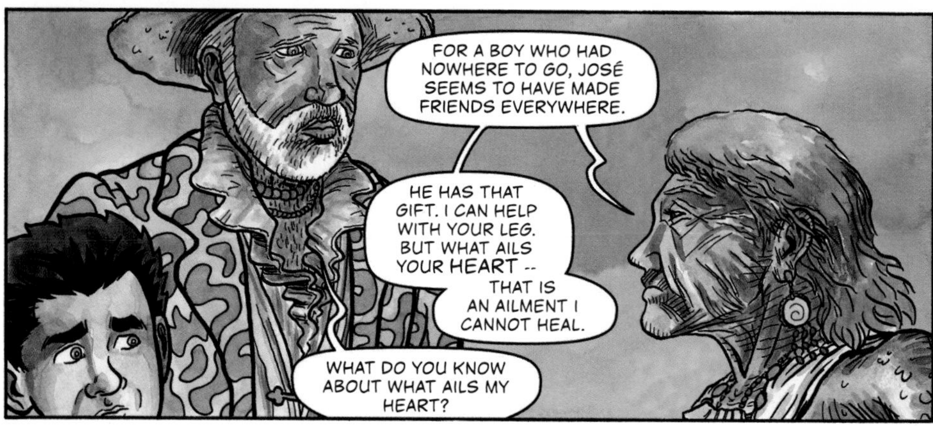
FOR A BOY WHO HAD NOWHERE TO GO, JOSÉ SEEMS TO HAVE MADE FRIENDS EVERYWHERE.
HE HAS THAT GIFT. I CAN HELP WITH YOUR LEG. BUT WHAT AILS YOUR HEART --
THAT IS AN AILMENT I CANNOT HEAL.
WHAT DO YOU KNOW ABOUT WHAT AILS MY HEART?

I KNOW THE PAIN THE SPANISH CAN BRING. MOST OF MY NATION IS ALREADY DEAD.
I AM SICK TOO.
I AM DYING.
OW!
LIE STILL!
THIS DISEASE CAME FROM ACROSS THE SEA.

FROM SPAIN.
WHY ARE YOU HELPING US?
BECAUSE YOUNG ROSA SAID THAT I WOULD.

SHE IS NOT LIKE THE OTHERS. SHE COMES TO TAKE CARE OF ME.
AH! WHAT ARE YOU DOING TO MY LEG?
THE BONE IS NOT BROKEN, BUT THE WOUND IS DEEP. IF I DO NOT CLOSE IT, IT WILL FESTER.
STOP WRIGGLING! THINK OF SOMETHING ELSE!

SOMETHING ELSE . . .
WAS ROSA THE GIRL IN THE JAIL?

SHE LIKES YOU, JOSÉ!

CACICA!
HUFF
IS JOSÉ STILL --
OH, THERE YOU ARE!
ROSA! DID YOU JUST RUN ALL THIS WAY?

I'M SO SORRY, JOSÉ. I WANTED TO CATCH YOU BEFORE YOU DISAPPEARED . . .
TO TELL YOU . . .

TO TELL YOU THAT YOUR FATHER IS DEAD.

I ALWAYS LIKED YOUR FATHER. HE WOULD GIVE ME CHUNKS OF SUGARCANE TO CHEW.
JUST BEFORE DE GUZMAN CAME FOR US, HE TOLD ME THAT WE'RE JEWS.

I KNEW WE CAME FROM PORTUGAL, BUT HE NEVER TOLD ME . . . UNTIL THE END, HE NEVER TOLD ME THAT WE WERE EXPELLED.
EXPELLED BY CHRISTIANS . . .

AND I THOUGHT I WAS ONE OF THEM!

YOU'RE LUCKY YOU AREN'T, JOSÉ.
I WISH I HAD A SECRET IDENTITY.

I'M SORRY! I . . . YOU'RE NOT LIKE THEM, ROSA.
YOU HAVE A SECRET IDENTITY. YOU HELP THE PEOPLE THEY HURT.

MIN HASHAMAYIM TENUHAMU.*
IT MEANS --
*MAY YOU BE COMFORTED FROM HEAVEN.

I KNOW WHAT IT MEANS!
IT IS WHAT WE SAY.

HOLD STILL.

MY SHIRT!
RRRIP!

IT IS WHAT WE DO.

THERE IS MORE THAT A JEW MUST DO TO MOURN THE DEATH OF HIS FATHER, BUT THE *LAQISH* WILL LEAVE HER COVE SOON.
IF SHE HAS NOT LEFT ALREADY.

BID YOUR FAREWELLS.

I'LL MISS YOU. I'M GLAD YOU'RE STILL WEARING IT.
I WON'T TAKE IT OFF UNTIL YOU COME BACK!
I CAN NEVER RETURN TO SANTO DOMINGO.

THE INQUISITION WILL END SOMEDAY. WE'LL SEE EACH OTHER AGAIN.

HURRY UP, JOSÉ!
I'M COMING!

WHAT IS THE FASTEST WAY TO THE COVE?
FOLLOW ME!

THE *CACICA* WORKED A MIRACLE ON YOUR LEG!
THE HERBS MAKE IT NUMB. IT WILL HURT AGAIN WHEN THE MEDICINE WEARS OFF.
I HOPE TO REACH THE SHIP BEFORE THEN.

THERE SHE IS!

WE'RE TOO LATE!
NOT YET! FOLLOW ME!

GRAB THAT VINE!

IT'S THE CAPTAIN!
AND JOSÉ!
THE BOY SAVED HIM!

HUZZAH!
HUZZAH!

WE MADE IT!
ARE YOU OKAY?
THE *CACICA'S* MEDICINE IS WEARING OFF.
HELP ME STAND.

WELCOME BACK!
WE SHOULD HAVE FOUGHT FOR YOU!
A LEGENDARY PERFORMANCE!
THE KID IS DEFINITELY A PIRATE NOW!
SO GLAD TO SEE YOU!
MOST HEROIC THING I'VE EVER SEEN!

SILENCE!
WHERE IS THE DOCTOR?
WHO HELD COMMAND IN MY ABSENCE?
HE LEFT US.
SAID HE'D BE NO USE TO US WITH HIS HAND LIKE IT WAS.

WELCOME BACK, CAPTAIN.
ERM . . .
THE SHIP IS YOURS AGAIN.
OF COURSE.

TELL THEM WHAT HE DID!
NOT YET.

LET THE MAINSAILS FILL WITH WIND!
THE *SANTA CLARA* IS AS GOOD AS OURS!

TAKE ME TO MY CABIN. AND SEND FOR THE TURNCOAT!

KNOCK KNOCK

YOU CALLED FOR ME, CAPTAIN.

YES. I WILL SPEAK WITH YOU.
ALONE.

SLAM!

JOSÉ!
WHERE IS THAT KID?

YOU'RE MISSING THE PARTY!

YOU ARE A TRAITOR!
SO WHY ARE YOU KEEPING ME ALIVE?

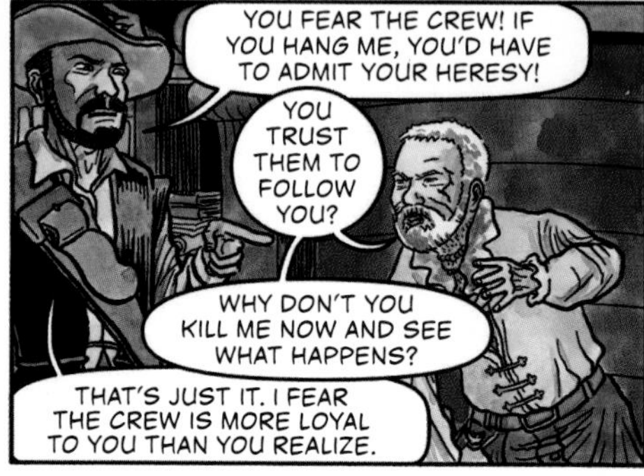
YOU FEAR THE CREW! IF YOU HANG ME, YOU'D HAVE TO ADMIT YOUR HERESY!
YOU TRUST THEM TO FOLLOW YOU?
WHY DON'T YOU KILL ME NOW AND SEE WHAT HAPPENS?
THAT'S JUST IT. I FEAR THE CREW IS MORE LOYAL TO YOU THAN YOU REALIZE.

. . .THEN THE CAPTAIN GRABBED A VINE --
WHAT A STORY!

AYE, AND WHAT A CAPTAIN! HE SAW SOMETHING IN YE WHEN ALL WE COULD SEE WAS A STOWAWAY.

SO WE HAVE REACHED A STALEMATE.
YOUR FEAR OF THE CREW'S FAITH KEEPS ME ALIVE.
MY FEAR OF THEIR LOYALTY KEEPS YOU IN COMMAND.

TO THE CAPTAIN!
AND JOSÉ!

A SAIL!
TO THE WEST! A SAIL!

The Santa Clara

THAT ACCURSED SHIP! WE MUSTN'T LET HER SLIP OUR GRASP THIS TIME!
SHE RIDES HIGH IN THE WATER -- THERE IS NOT MUCH CARGO IN HER.
THERE IS NOT MUCH BETWEEN YOUR EARS!
SHE'S A SHIP OF THE SPANISH NAVY! THERE'S ALWAYS GOLD ON THOSE!

WHAT IS OUR SPEED?
SEVEN KNOTS, SIR!
WE'LL CATCH HER!

I DON'T LIKE THE LOOK OF THOSE CLOUDS . . .
TRIM THE SAILS! WE CAN GO FASTER.

CAPTAIN! WE'VE GOT HER!
AT LAST!
AFTER ALL THESE YEARS!

SIR, BEFORE WE GO INTO BATTLE, I'D LIKE TO CLEAR THE AIR WITH YE, IF I MAY.

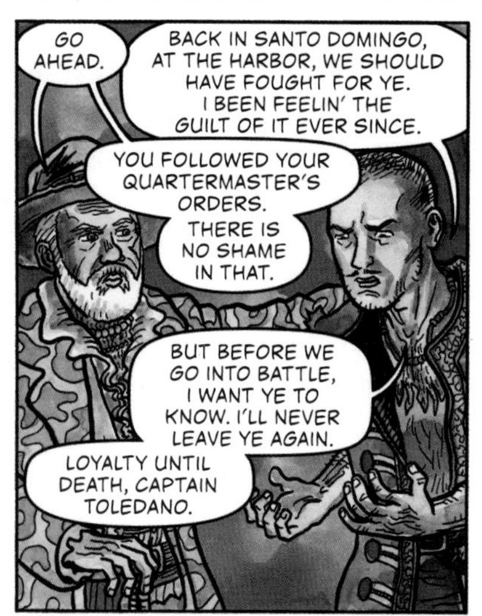
GO AHEAD.
BACK IN SANTO DOMINGO, AT THE HARBOR, WE SHOULD HAVE FOUGHT FOR YE. I BEEN FEELIN' THE GUILT OF IT EVER SINCE.
YOU FOLLOWED YOUR QUARTERMASTER'S ORDERS.
THERE IS NO SHAME IN THAT.
BUT BEFORE WE GO INTO BATTLE, I WANT YE TO KNOW. I'LL NEVER LEAVE YE AGAIN.
LOYALTY UNTIL DEATH, CAPTAIN TOLEDANO.

LOYALTY UNTIL DEATH!
CALL TO STATIONS! PREPARE FOR BATTLE!

NO!

LOOK AT THOSE CLOUDS!
THAT'S THE BIGGEST STORM WE'VE SEEN IN MONTHS!

IF WE DON'T SINK THE *SANTA CLARA*, THAT STORM WILL. AND IF WE PURSUE HER, WE MAY SINK TOO!

BUT THE GOLD --
YOU THINK THIS IS ABOUT GOLD?

THIS HAS NOTHING TO DO WITH GOLD!
ASK YOUR CAPTAIN!

CAREFUL, SIR!
OR YOU WILL REGRET WHAT YOU SAY!
I ONLY SAY THE TRUTH!
THE CAPTAIN OF THE *SANTA CLARA* IS AN AGENT OF THE INQUISITION!
I DON'T UNDERSTAND.
SHUT UP!
HIS FATHER WAS THE GRAND INQUISITOR WHO PUT OUR DEAR CAPTAIN'S FAMILY TO DEATH.
YOU'VE SAID ENOUGH!

OUR CAPTAIN IS A HERETIC!
A *MARRANO!*
A JEW!

SAY SOMETHING!

WHAT IS THERE TO SAY? OUR CAPTAIN HAS BEEN LYING TO US ALL THESE YEARS. HAVE YOU NEVER WONDERED WHY WE ONLY PLUNDER FROM SPANISH SHIPS?
AND NOW?
HE WASTES OUR TIME PURSUING A PRIZE THAT IS NO PRIZE AT ALL.
THERE IS NO GOLD FOR US ON THE *SANTA CLARA*!
ONLY THE JEW'S PERSONAL VENDETTA!

NO GOLD?
WHAT'S HE SAYING?

IT'S NOT JUST A VENDETTA!
JOSÉ! DON'T!

MY FATHER IS DEAD BECAUSE OF THE CAPTAIN OF THAT SHIP!
THEY TOOK HIM BECAUSE HE . . .
BECAUSE WE ARE JEWS!

I AM A JEW TOO.

YOU SEE? THE CAPTAIN BROUGHT ANOTHER ONE ONTO OUR SHIP AND MADE HIM HIS FAVORITE!
I ASK YOU, IS THIS FAIR?
WE SPENT YEARS AT SEA PURSUING THE *SANTA CLARA!* WHAT FOR?

AND ALL THIS TIME, GOD HAS FROWNED UPON US FOR TAKING ORDERS FROM A HERETIC!

I, TOO, AM A JEW!

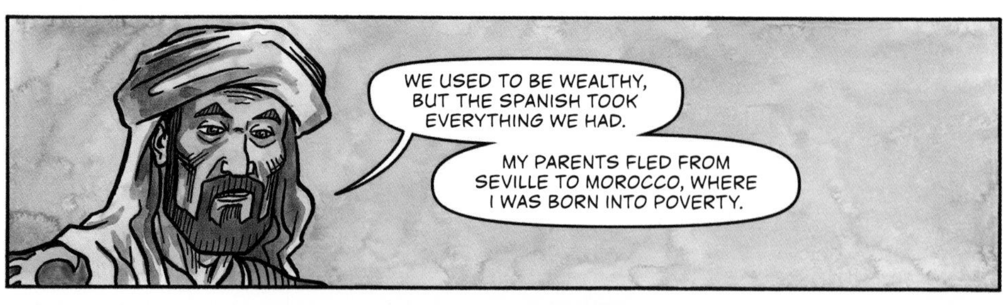
WE USED TO BE WEALTHY, BUT THE SPANISH TOOK EVERYTHING WE HAD.
MY PARENTS FLED FROM SEVILLE TO MOROCCO, WHERE I WAS BORN INTO POVERTY.

I AM NOT A JEW, BUT --
MY FAMILY WAS KILLED BY THE PORTUGUESE, AND I WAS SOLD AS A SLAVE TO THE SPANIARDS.
IF THE CAPTAIN WISHES REVENGE, I SHARE HIS WISH.

I SHARE IT TOO!
MY FAMILY WERE PRINCES IN ANDALUSIA, AND LOYAL SERVANTS OF THE PROPHET. WE STILL SERVE THE PROPHET, BUT OUR KINGDOM IS GONE.

ME PARENTS WERE KILLED FOR WORSHIPING THE PAGAN GODS.
MY FATHER WAS A TAINO MAN. HE WAS KILLED BY COLONISTS WHEN THEY FOUND OUT.
I'M . . . I'M SPANISH . . . BUT THIS ALL SOUNDS SO AWFUL!
I WISH I COULD BE SOMETHING ELSE!

DON'T SAY THAT!
WE ARE WHO WE ARE --
WE SHOULDN'T BE PUNISHED FOR THAT.

BUT THAT -- THAT'S IT!
AREN'T YOU PUNISHING THOSE POOR SAILORS ON THE *SANTA CLARA* JUST FOR WHO THEY ARE?

NO.

MEN ON THE *SANTA CLARA* HAVE KILLED INNOCENT PEOPLE.
THE SHIP ITSELF WAS PAID FOR WITH MONEY THEY PLUNDERED FROM JEWS AND MOORS AND ANYONE ELSE THEY DIDN'T LIKE.

THE INQUISITION IS NOT JUST A MOMENT IN HISTORY.
IT HAS BEEN GOING ON FOR HALF A CENTURY.
IT CONTINUES TO THIS DAY.
THEY ARE ITS AGENTS.

AND SO ARE YOU!

CAPTAIN! SHE'S COMING IN RANGE!

LASH HIM TO THE MAST!
WAIT! NO! WHAT ARE YOU DOING?!
MUSTER TO STATIONS! MAN THE CANNONS!

UNBIND ME, YOU HEATHENS!
WHAT WILL YOU DO WITH HIM?

THIS IS NOT THE TIME TO DECIDE. HOW WELL HAVE YOU LEARNED YOUR ROPES?
MY ROPES?

BIND ME TO THE GUNWALE!

I CAN HARDLY STAND, BUT I WILL COMMAND THIS BATTLE.

WHAT ABOUT ME?
THIS IS YOUR FIGHT AS MUCH AS IT IS MINE.
TAKE MY SWORD.

MAKE SURE THAT SHIP AND HER CAPTAIN NEVER SEE LAND AGAIN!
GUNS AT THE READY!

FIRE!

BOOM

CRASH!
SPLASH!
SPLASH!

RETURN FIRE!!

TAKE COVER!!

HIT THEM AGAIN! BEFORE THEY RELOAD!

BOOM!
BOOM!

WE GOT HER!

SHE HAS NO RUDDER! BRING US CLOSE AND PREPARE THE GRAPPLES!

AWAY THE HOOKS!

YOU!

THE BEAN COUNTER'S KID.

NOT SO FAST, PIP-SQUEAK.

HAVE YOU COME FOR REVENGE?

NOT REVENGE!
I'VE COME FOR JUSTICE!

HA!

YOU'VE COME TO DIE, HERETIC! GOD IS ON MY SIDE!

WHOA!

YIELD.

GO AHEAD, DO YOUR WORST!
THE INQUISITION WILL LIVE ON, AND YOU WILL BE LIKE A RABBIT IN THE WOODS, FOREVER AFRAID OF THE WOLVES IN THE NIGHT.

HURRY! THE STORM IS TOO CLOSE!

GO ON, JOSÉ. KILL HIM!
NO! TIE HIM TO THE MAST!

I'D RATHER YOU KILL ME!
THE INQUISITION WILL RALLY AROUND MY NAME!

I'LL BE MUCH MORE POWERFUL IF YOU KILL ME!
I WON'T KILL YOU.

BUT I'LL MAKE SURE THE STORM WILL.
ALL ANYONE WILL KNOW IS THAT YOU WERE LOST AT SEA. WILL THE INQUISITION TAKE REVENGE AGAINST THE CLOUDS?

GRAB THE QUARTERMASTER!
HE SHOULD JOIN HIS LOT!

HELP!
ROSA?!

JOSÉ!
OVER HERE!

ROSA!
THE KEYS?
THERE!
THEY BLAMED ME FOR YOUR CAPTAIN'S ESCAPE!
THEY'RE TAKING ME TO THE INQUISITION COURT!

THEY AREN'T TAKING YOU ANYWHERE!

ANY SIGN OF HIM?
THERE!

JOSÉ!
HELP!

RUN! HURRY!

CAST OFF THE GRAPPLES! OR WE'LL GO DOWN WITH HER!

LAQISH

LAQISH

LAQISH

YOUR FRIEND ROSA IS A REMARKABLE HEALER. MY LEG FEELS MUCH BETTER.

THAT'S NICE.
COME. YOU SHOULD JOIN THE CELEBRATION.
I DON'T FEEL LIKE CELEBRATING.

THEN COME FOR ANOTHER REASON. IT IS TIME YOU EMBRACE WHO YOU ARE.

QUIET, MY FRIENDS.
GATHER ROUND.

FOR YEARS, WE PURSUED DE GUZMAN AND HIS SHIP.

AND WITH JOSÉ'S HELP, WE GOT THEM!

BUT WE DID NOT END THE INQUISITION.
IN THE OLD WORLD AND IN THE NEW, THE LAND IS STILL NOT SAFE FOR US.

FOR MANY YEARS, JOSÉ'S FATHER USED THIS CUP TO RECITE A PRAYER ON FRIDAY NIGHTS. ALWAYS IN SECRET, AND IN SILENCE.
TODAY IS YET ANOTHER FRIDAY. THIS NIGHT IS, ONCE AGAIN, OUR *SHABBAT*, OUR DAY OF REST. ON LAND, THE SILENCE PERSISTS. JEWS IN SPANISH LANDS DO NOT DARE UTTER THESE WORDS ALOUD.

BUT, JOSÉ, BECAUSE OF YOU, WE ARE FREE TO RAISE OUR VOICES ON THE SEA.
IT IS TIME FOR YOU TO HEAR THE WORDS YOUR FATHER RECITED.

יום השישי...
YOM HASHISHI . . .
JE '21

Historical Note

In 1492, on the very day of Columbus's departure, the Edict of the Expulsion of the Jews took effect in Spain. It ordered all Jews to leave Spain forever -- or face terrible consequences. Some Spanish Jews escaped to the sea, including members of Columbus's expedition. So, were there really Jewish pirates? Historians debate this question, but you can look up Samuel Palache, Moses Cohen Henriques, Sinan Reis, or Yaacov Kuriel and decide for yourself.

About the Author

Arnon Z. Shorr is a filmmaker and screenwriter. He grew up between worlds: half Sefaradi and half Ashkenazi, a Hebrew speaker living in America, a Jewish private-school kid in a mostly non-Jewish suburb. Whenever he'd set foot in one world, his other foot would betray him as *different*. That's why he tells stories that embrace the peculiar, where things that are different are the keys to survival and success. If you'd like to learn more about Arnon, his book, films, and screenplays, visit www.arnonshorr.com.

About the Illustrator

Joshua M. Edelglass is the assistant director of Camp Ramah New England. His illustrations have appeared in a variety of newspapers and magazines, and he illustrated stories for *The Jewish Comix Anthology*, published by Alternate History Comics. His artwork has appeared in numerous exhibitions, including *Pow! Jewish Comics Art and Influence* (Brooklyn, 2018); *JOMIX -- Jewish Comics: Art and Derivation* (New York & Philadelphia, 2016); and *The Jew as the Other* (New York, 2015). Joshua's writings about movies, television, comic books, and more can be found at www.JoshuaEdelglass.com.

Acknowledgments

We could not have made this book without help, guidance, and support from many people, including (but not limited to) Avigail Appelbaum-Charnov, for historical architecture guidance; Kate Farrell, for pitch notes and support; Joanne Lewis, for notes on Taino history and culture; Richard Rasner, for all things Pirate; and the entire cast and crew of *The Pirate Captain Toledano* for making the film that led to this book. A special tip of the hat to Diana Haberstick (CDG), whose original costume designs for the film inspired some of the clothing illustrations here, and to Stephen DeCordova, who gave Captain Toledano his face and voice. Thank you to our agent, Anna Olswanger, who was first to recognize this book's potential. We also thank Joni Sussman, along with Viet, Danielle, Taylor, and the teams at Kar-Ben and Lerner for being such supportive partners. Josh would like to thank Rabbi Ed Gelb and the entire Camp Ramah New England team, for being so supportive and helping him to find the extra time he needed to complete his work on this book. Josh is also deeply grateful to Steph, Tahlia, and Reya for their love and their understanding of the many, many hours he spent hiding away in the basement, drawing! And Arnon thanks Talia, Adir, Ilana, and Margalit, who let him write in peace (in the walk-in closet) during the first weeks of the COVID lockdown.